Pirate Stories

Another book from Macmillan

PIRATE POEMS
by David Harmer

Kate Pankhurst illustrates children's books from
her Liverpool-based studio. She has a particular
passion for finding peculiar-looking people and
animals to draw and is pleased that this has led to
a very exciting job as an illustrator.

Pirate Stories

Chosen by Emma Young

Illustrated by Kate Pankhurst

MACMILLAN CHILDREN'S BOOKS

For Captain Louis and Pirate Angelo

First published 2007 by Macmillan Children's Books
an imprint of Pan Macmillan
20 New Wharf Road, London N1 9RR
Associated companies throughout the world
www.panmacmillan.com

ISBN 978-0-330-45148-2

19 18

A CIP catalogue record for this book is available from
the British Library.

Typeset by Nigel Hazle
Printed and bound by CPI Group (UK) Ltd, Croydon, CR0 4YY

Contents

Pirates Win Prizes

Vic Parker

'Once again, lads!' Captain Cutlass cried. He was standing on the deck of the *Blue Moon*, his entire pirate crew in neat rows in front of him. 'And this time, you ugly bunch of barnacles, sing it with feeling!' he roared.

'With feeling! With feeling!' squawked Pineapple Poll the parrot, perched on one of the cannons.

The pirates grumbled. It was the third time that day that Captain Cutlass had called them for sea-shanty singing practice – and it

2

was only eleven in the morning!
But the captain was ruthless — there
was nothing he wanted more than
to win this year's Stars of the Sea
Talent Competition. The contest
was the most important event in
the world pirating calendar. The
winners became hugely famous
overnight — even more famous
than the winners of the Seven
Seas Swashbuckling Knockout
Tournament or the Buccaneer
Booty Treasure Hunt. Photos of
the winning crew were plastered

all over the front page of the *Black Spot Bugle* (the number-one pirate newspaper), and the captain was interviewed by glamorous celebrity reporter Cat O'Ninetails herself. The winning artistes were booked to make regular appearances at the legendary Scurvy Dog Inn, favourite hangout of very great pirate heroes like Gentleman Jake, Bloodeye Bill and Doubloon Donna the Dangerous. And first prize meant more pieces of eight than a pirate could dream of! Gold came

rolling in from companies
like Gunbarrel Grog,
Swag Snacks and Yo
Ho Ho Shampoo,
who wanted to have
the winners' faces on
their products.

Yes, every
pirate captain
worth his sea salt wanted to win
first prize in the Stars of the Sea
Talent Competition, and Captain
Cutlass and the crew of the *Blue
Moon* always tried their hardest to

succeed. One year they had shown off their knot-tying skills – but got tangled up in their own rigging! Another year they had performed card tricks – but got into a fight when another crew accused them of cheating! Last year, they had told jokes . . .

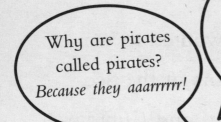

Why are pirates called pirates? *Because they aaarrrrrr!*

How much did it cost the pirate captain for his hook and his wooden stump? *An arm and a leg!*

. . . but the judges had heard them all before.

Unsurprisingly, poor old Captain Cutlass and his crew had always come away empty-handed. But this year he was determined that his men's singing would shiver the judges' timbers. The pirates knew that if they didn't get their sea shanty shipshape by the time they arrived for the competition at Dead Man's Bay, Captain Cutlass would tie their bootlaces together and throw them all overboard — without their water wings.

'Again!' Captain Cutlass

commanded. 'And this time I want to hear the melodies of mermaids instead of you rowdy rabble!'

'Rowdy rabble! Rowdy rabble!' screeched Pineapple Poll, flapping out of the way as Captain Cutlass swiped his conductor's baton at her. She settled herself safely out of reach as the captain rapped his baton sharply on the rail. Then the pirates began to sing:

'*My Bonny lies over the ocean*
My Bonny lies over the sea

My Bonny lies over the ocean
O bring back my Bonny to me.'

There was a flash of colour as Pineapple Poll swooped down to join in with the chorus. '*Bring back, bring back, O bring back my Bonny to me, to me,'* she trilled, swinging her tail feathers to the tune. '*Bring back, bring back, O bring back my Bonny to me.'*

'Will someone shut that parrot up!' roared Captain Cutlass in a fury. 'How am I expected to keep everyone in time when that good-for-nothing bird keeps butting in?'

Flat-Foot Fred and Scarface Stan picked up an empty gunpowder keg and dropped it over Pineapple Poll. 'Shh,' Fred whispered through the wood. 'Don't annoy the captain or he'll have you made into a feather duster quicker than you can say Davy Jones's locker.'

'Davy Jones's locker!' squawked a small, mournful voice from deep inside the barrel.

Luckily, Captain Cutlass didn't

hear. He was already rousing the pirates for one more chorus. And as the *Blue Moon* cut through the sea, full speed ahead for Dead Man's Bay, their gruff voices boomed out over the waves:

'*My Bonny lies over the ocean . . .*'

Captain Cutlass kept his crew practising morning, noon and night. He even made them rehearse while they performed their duties. The pirates sang melodies while they mended the mainsail. They hummed harmonies while they swabbed the decks. They crooned choruses while keeping a lookout in the crow's-nest.

It took two long weeks for the *Blue Moon* to reach the calm waters of Dead Man's Bay – and by the morning of the competition, the pirates had sung themselves quite hoarse. Their throats were so sore from all the practising that, when they tried to sing, no more than squeaks and croaks came out! Captain Cutlass couldn't believe his hairy ears. In a panic, he ordered

all the pirates to wrap up in their
thickest skull-and-crossbones scarves.
He made each of them swallow a
double dose of Make Me Hearty
medicine. Finally, he forced them

all to gargle with sea-water. But nothing made a difference: in fact, the poor pirates just ended up feeling sick as well as sore.

'You useless load of landlubbers!' Captain Cutlass raged, hopping mad. 'We can't even enter the talent contest now – let alone win it! We'd be the joke of the oceans! We'd be the laughing stock of the seas! Curse and confound it! Winning that competition would have been the feather in my cap –' Suddenly he stopped. A glint came

14

into his eye. He scratched his beard and thought for a moment. Then he threw back his head and chuckled. 'Yes,' he smirked. 'That's not a bad idea at all.'

The pale-faced pirates looked at each other in bewilderment.

'Well, don't just stand there gawping!' Captain Cutlass bellowed. 'The competition's about to start.'

Captain Cutlass and the crew of the *Blue Moon* joined hundreds of eager contestants thronging the sandy shore. The finest pirate crews in all the seven seas had come from far and wide to take part. A mighty cheer went up as the three judges took their places under a palm tree: Captain Cowell, Sharkbite Sharon and Peg-Leg Louis. It was time for the battle to begin.

First, Pistol Pedro and the crew of the *Fair Spanish Lady* put on an amazing display of juggling with coconuts.

'It's not as if the coconuts were blazing cannonballs,' sneered

16

Captain Cowell. '*That* would have been exciting.'

Next, Chow Yun Li from the *Demon Dragon* did a magic trick. He took one of Sharkbite Sharon's gold neck-chains and made it vanish before the judges' eyes. Unfortunately, he couldn't bring it back again.

'Disqualified!' roared Sharkbite Sharon, leaping to her feet in a fury, and Chow Yun Li fled as fast as his legs could carry him.

Then came Cut-Throat Kate and the all-girl crew of the *Saucy Sue*.

They walked the plank and did soaring dives into the waves below before performing an elegant water ballet.

'Boring, boring, boring!' yawned Peg-Leg Louis. 'Shame the waters weren't infested with stingrays – that would have spiced things up a bit . . . Next!'

One by one, the pirate acts took their turn. And one by one, they were jeered off the beach by the judges. Then came the last announcement: 'And finally, ladies and gents, we have a representative from the *Blue Moon,* singing a sea shanty.'

Captain Cutlass tried not to bite his nails as out on to the sand strode – Pineapple Poll. For a second or two, the crew of the *Blue Moon* sat in stunned silence. Then they sprang to their feet and clapped as loudly as they could, to make up for the fact that they couldn't cheer. Gasps of surprise rippled through the pirate audience. The three judges sat bolt upright in anticipation.

'A ship's parrot!' exclaimed

19

Sharkbite Sharon. 'Now there's something we haven't seen before.'

'Very modern . . . very different,' agreed Captain Cowell.

'Interesting,' murmured Peg-Leg Louis. 'I wish I'd thought of it!'

Everyone fell silent as Pineapple Poll began to sing in her best, most beautiful, clear, sweet voice.

'*My Bonny lies over the ocean*
My Bonny lies over the sea
My Bonny lies over the ocean
O bring back my bonny to me.'

By the time the parrot reached the chorus, there was a tear in every pirate's eye. Even the icy Captain Cowell was reaching for his neckerchief.

'*Bring back, bring back, O bring back my Bonny to me,*' finished Pineapple Poll eventually, as sadly and movingly as she could.

Thunderous applause rang out across the bay. The pirate audience cheered and stamped their feet. 'More!' they shouted. 'Encore! Encore!'

21

'That's my girl!' Captain Cutlass bellowed, grinning from ear to ear. 'I always knew she could do it!'

Poll's feathery chest swelled with pride as she fanned out her multicoloured wings and prepared to sing again . . .

Of course, Pineapple Poll was declared the winner. And, by the time the *Blue Moon* sailed away from Dead Man's Bay, the coveted first prize was proudly on display at the top of the mast – the gold Stars of the Sea winner's flag fluttering for all to see.

Captain Cutlass held a fantastic celebration banquet. There was rum-and-raisin ice cream to soothe his crew's poorly throats, with rum-baked bananas, rum truffles and rum-baba cakes — all washed down with plenty of rum. And, for the guest of honour, there was as much pineapple as Poll could eat.

'We're the Stars of the Sea!' she squawked. 'The Stars of the Sea!'

'That's right,' beamed Captain

23

Cutlass. 'And we're going to make sure it stays that way. Now listen, everyone. For next year's competition, I thought we'd all dance the hornpipe. Let's get practising!'

Pirate Girl

Cornelia Funke

Captain Firebeard was the terror of
the high seas. His ship, the *Horrible
Haddock*, sailed faster than the
wind over the waves. Whenever
the *Horrible Haddock* appeared on
the horizon, the knees of honest
seafaring folk would shake like jelly.

Captain Firebeard had a fearsome crew. His helmsman was Morgan O'Meany. His cook was Cutlass Tom. Not forgetting Bill the Bald, Willy Wooden-Hand, Crooked Carl and twenty more terrible pirates just like them.

When Firebeard's crew boarded a ship, nothing was safe. They stole the silver spoons and the captain's uniform. They stole the ship's figurehead, the pots and pans, the hammocks and the sails. And, of course, they stole ALL the casks of rum.

But one day Firebeard robbed
a ship that he should have left
well alone. On board was a little
girl called Molly, who was off on
holiday to see her granny.

The pirates leaped on board
with an ear-splitting roar. Molly
tried hiding among the ropes, but
Morgan O'Meany soon fished her
out.

'What shall we do with her?' he
smirked.

'Take her with us, you fool!'
bellowed Firebeard. 'Her parents

will pay a handsome ransom for
such a little treasure. And if not,
then we'll feed her to the sharks.'

'You'll be sorry for this!' cried
Molly.

But Morgan O'Meany rolled her
up like a herring and tossed her on
board the *Horrible Haddock*.

When the sun had gone down,
Bill the Bald dragged Molly to see
the captain.

'Right, tell me your parents'
names and address, or else!' growled
Captain Firebeard.

'Will not!' Molly growled back.
'If I told you my mother's name,
you'd be so scared, you'd cry like a
baby!'

At this, all the pirates howled
with laughter.

So Molly was put to work. She
peeled potatoes and cleaned boots.
She polished cutlasses, patched sails
and scrubbed the deck. Soon every
bone in her body ached.

Three times a day Firebeard
asked her, 'Name and address?'

But Molly just smiled.

'Feed her to the sharks!' roared Willy Wooden-Hand. But Firebeard ground his teeth and said, 'She'll talk before long.'

Every night the pirates had a party. They drank rum, staggered across the deck, danced on the ship's rigging and bawled out the rudest songs.

But Molly had a plan. While the pirates were carousing, she wrote secret messages and popped them

30

into empty
bottles. When
the pirates were
safely snoring in
their bunks, she
tossed them into the

sea. Molly did this every night.

One night the pirates partied until
dawn. But this time, they fell asleep
on the deck. Molly tiptoed over the
tangle of arms and legs, and threw
her bottle over the ship's rail. *Splish!*
Splash! It landed in the deep, wide
sea.

'Hey! What was that?' yelled Morgan O'Meany. The pirates staggered over to the rail.

'It's a message in a bottle!' they all cried.

'Bring it to me!' shouted Captain Firebeard. 'Now!'

The pirates dived to the bottom of the sea. They searched and searched, but Molly's message had bobbed away. Soaking wet, they crawled back on deck, cursing.

'Tell me what you wrote!' demanded Captain Firebeard.

But Molly just kicked at his wooden leg.

Firebeard went as red as a lobster. 'NOW it's time to feed her to the sharks!' he roared.

But a cry from above stopped him. 'P-P-P-Pirates!' shouted Ten-Pint Ted from the crow's-nest.

'Nonsense!' scoffed Firebeard. '*We're* the only pirates around here.'

But he was wrong. A ship with red sails was speeding towards them. A giant black flag with a skull and crossbones fluttered from its mast.

33

'Who in the name of Neptune's beard is that?' stuttered Firebeard.

'That's my mum!' grinned Molly.

'It's Barbarous Bertha herself!' wailed the crew of the *Horrible Haddock*.

Firebeard went as white as a sheet and his pirates rolled their eyes in fear. This time it was their knees that were shaking. And Bill the Bald's false teeth almost flew out of his mouth.

The ship with the red sails drew closer and closer. Barbarous Bertha

34

stood at the prow, swinging her cutlass.

'Wait until she sees my hands!' said Molly. 'They're red and raw from peeling potatoes. That will make my mum maddest of all!'

Firebeard and his pirates groaned with terror.

Soon Barbarous Bertha was alongside the *Horrible Haddock*. Her ferocious crew swung themselves over the rail with a terrible roar.

'We're here at last, my pirate girl!' cried Barbarous Bertha,

throwing Molly up high into the
air. 'We got your message. Your
granny was beginning to wonder
where you were. Now, how
nasty can we be to these piratical
nincompoops?'

'Well!' said Molly. 'That's easy.'

From that day on, Captain
Firebeard and his pirate crew had
no time to think about raiding ships.

Willy Wooden-Hand scrubbed
the deck. Morgan O'Meany and
Cutlass Tom peeled vegetables

36

from morning until night. Captain
Firebeard polished Barbarous
Bertha's boots fourteen times a
week.

And Molly was finally able to
visit her granny!

Uncle Jolly Roger

John Grant

Jim stood at the window of his gran's cottage. Outside was a lawn. Beyond the lawn was a fence. And beyond the fence were a low cliff and the sea. In a few days it would be Christmas. When Dad said that he had to go to Paris for a day or two on business, Mum said, 'I'll come too, and do some Christmas shopping. Jim can stay with Gran.'

This sounded like an excellent plan to Jim. He wanted to ask about Uncle Roger, a member of the family no one spoke about. He had lived a long time ago, and was so wicked that his family had been ashamed of him (and they still were). But whenever Jim tried to find out the terrible secret, Dad said, 'You don't want to know about such things.' But of course

Jim wanted to know, and surely Gran would tell him. She knew lots of family stories, and some of them were even true.

Jim's older cousin Dan had told him a bit about Uncle Roger. 'He was a very wicked young man,' he'd said. 'I think perhaps he was a highwayman, robbing stage coaches. My dad said he was arrested for something, but escaped and ran away to sea and never came back.'

Jim asked Gran on the first day

of his visit. She said, 'He must have been amusing company. He was nicknamed "Jolly Roger". In any case, he was not from my side of the family. We were always very respectable.'

Perhaps he was a pirate, thought Jim.

He said so to Gran's green budgie, Joey. But, as he always did when Jim spoke to him, Joey cocked his head and said, 'Joey's a good boy!'

Jim went to bed thinking about Jolly Roger. If he *was* a pirate, did

he have a wooden leg? Or a hook?
Or a parrot on his shoulder?

A few hours later, pale sunshine
shone through the window as Jim
came slowly awake. That was odd.
His window faced north. And this
strange light wasn't bright enough
to be sunshine. Suddenly, a voice
cried out and caused him to sit up in
bed. 'Show a leg, Jim lad! The tide's
on the turn and the wind stands fair
for a voyage to the islands and the
treasure of Elmo the Mighty!'

Jim jumped out of bed and

switched on the light. There was a
face at the window! For a moment
Jim was frozen to the spot. He
couldn't move. Looking through
the glass was a cheerful gentleman
dressed in old-fashioned clothes and
holding aloft a flickering lantern.
He had a black beard, a patch over
one eye, and a parrot sitting on his
shoulder.

Jim pushed the window open.
'Who are you?' he asked.

The man laughed. 'Me? I'm your
great-great-something-or-other-

uncle. You're to be my cabin boy.
Get your sea-boots and your parrot!'

'You are Uncle Jolly Roger!' cried
Jim as he dressed. He tucked his
jeans into his wellies, turning down
the rubber tops like pirate boots
he had seen in books. Now for a

parrot. He hurried
into the sitting
room. 'Joey,'
he said, 'you're
going to sea.'
Half asleep, Joey
muttered, 'Joey's a

good boy!' as Jim carried him back to his bedroom and climbed out through the window.

Uncle Jolly Roger was already striding across the lawn. They climbed over the fence and down a steep path to the beach, where a longboat was drawn up at the water's edge. In a moment they were aboard and skimming across the waves towards a large three-masted ship lying at anchor.

As they boarded this second ship, Uncle Roger shouted, 'Up anchor!

Make sail! Course west-sou'-west!'
Jim looked back. There was a bright
light on shore. His bedroom. He had
forgotten to switch off the light!

Day was breaking as the shore
disappeared from view. A man with
a wooden leg and a cook's hat
came on deck shouting, 'Breakfast!
Come and get it!'

In the captain's cabin Jim sat
down to a bowl of what the cook
who served it called 'burgoo'. 'Sailor
talk for porridge,' explained Uncle
Jolly Roger. There was also ship's

biscuit – bursting with weevils – to which Jim said, 'No, thank you.' (He had another helping of burgoo instead.)

When they had eaten, Uncle Roger spread a map on the cabin table. It showed an island with a cross marked on it in red ink. Beside the cross was written:

Here be the treasure of
Cap'n Elmo the Mighty.

'Captain Elmo: a small man with big ideas,' mused Uncle Roger. 'This is one of only two copies of the map. Black-Belt Dan has the other. He sailed with Captain Elmo and claims the treasure as his own.'

At that moment the parrot flew to the cabin window and screeched, 'Ship ahoy!' Joey joined in helpfully with, 'Joey's a good boy!'

Captain Roger took one look. 'Shiver me timbers!' he cried. ''Tis himself! My arch-rival, Black-Belt Dan!' A ship painted black all over and flaunting billowing black sails was coming up fast astern. The

captain hurried on deck, followed
by Jim. There was a puff of smoke
and a bang. A cannonball whizzed
overhead. 'Can't we go any faster?'
panicked Jim. 'No need,' said the
captain, smiling to himself. 'We
have a secret weapon.' He pointed
to a large brass cannon in the stern
and shouted, 'Load! Aim! FIRE!'

The smoke blew away. The black
ship drew closer.

'We missed!' cried Jim.

But as they watched, the black
sails began to flap wildly. The ship

was moving very slowly, swinging

one way then the other.

'There's no one steering,' said Jim.

'There's no one doing anything,'

smirked the captain. 'They're all too

busy stuffing themselves with wine

gums, jelly babies, sticky toffees and

chocolate drops. Black-Belt Dan

is very particular about feeding his

crew, you see: wholemeal bread,

skimmed milk, fresh vegetables. He

doesn't allow sweets on board. A

giant bag of mixed sweets bursting

in the rigging is better than ten

cannonballs. And when they've eaten all the sweets, most of the crew will be too sick to sail the ship.'

Then he shouted, 'Mister Mate, set all sails . . . every inch of canvas the masts will carry!' By noon the black ship was but a smudge on the horizon.

Dawn was breaking the next morning as Captain Roger's ship rode at anchor. A long boat ferried him and Jim, plus two spade-bearing sailors, on to a sandy beach.

Close by was a large boulder painted with a skull and crossbones.

The captain gave Jim the map. 'Read what's written, boy,' he instructed.

'From Dead Man's Rock,' said Jim, 'it is eighteen places sou'-west.'

The captain looked at his pocket compass and took eighteen steps to the south-west.

'Twenty paces nor'-nor'-west,' read Jim, and Captain Roger ploughed on until Jim called out, 'Twelve paces east-sou'-east, that's

53

the place!' The sailors took up
their spades and started to dig. But
only a few inches under the soil
they hit solid rock. There was no
way any treasure could be buried
here.

'This map's a fake!' bellowed
Captain Roger.

'I don't think so,' said Jim slowly.
'You told me that Elmo was a
small man. My size, perhaps. He
would have taken shorter strides,
like me.'

'Good thinking!' cried the captain.

54

'Let's try again. Back to Dead Man's Rock, everyone.'

And this time, with Jim pacing out the directions, they arrived at a patch of bare earth in the centre of a forest clearing. A few minutes' digging and a big, ironbound chest was on its way back to the ship.

On a dark, moonless night, Jim stepped ashore from the longboat. He carried his share of the treasure: two small bags of gold doubloons and a small silver coin he had

found in the forest clearing. He said

goodbye to his uncle and climbed

the cliff path. As he clambered over

the fence he saw a light in one of

the windows of Gran's cottage.

His bedroom. It was surprising that

Gran had not noticed the light. He

climbed in, closed the window and

returned Joey to his cage. He laid

the doubloons on the bedside table

before undressing, then switched

off the light and slipped under the

duvet.

Gran woke Jim in the morning

and exclaimed, 'How did you get
your boots so muddy? They're filthy!
And another thing — you'll spoil
them turning down the tops like
that.' She saw the gold doubloons.
'Ah! The chocolate coins for the
Christmas tree. I've been looking
for them everywhere. I wonder how
they got here?'

Jim was on the verge of telling
her all about Uncle Jolly Roger. But
would she believe it? He wasn't sure
if even he believed it. Perhaps it had
all been a dream.

He reached into his jeans pocket
and took out the silver coin. That
was real.

The Pirats

colin McNaughton

Ladies and gentlemen, our hero:
the incredible Anton B. Stanton, the
smallest boy in the whole history
of the world. He lived with his
normal-sized mum, his normal-sized
dad and his normal-sized brothers in
a normal-sized castle.

Being small was something Anton had grown used to. Indeed, being small had certain advantages: he often noticed things that other, bigger people would miss.

One hot and sticky summer

afternoon, Anton was taking a
cooling swim in the moat when he
saw something very strange hidden
among the reeds.

'Stone the crows!' said Anton. 'It's
a little ship!'

I wonder who this belongs to,
he thought. Maybe I should take a
look. He climbed aboard to explore.
The ship seemed to be deserted.
Suddenly he heard voices!

Too late to slip over the side,
Anton found an empty barrel and
clambered inside. As the voices

came closer he looked up. At the
top of the mast flew a rat skull and
crossbones. Anton B. Stanton froze
in horror. PIRATS!

'Trouble from the Water Rats!'
bellowed the first Pirat. 'You must
be joking – weak as water, all of
'em!'

'Ha ha, that's a good 'un!'
laughed the second. 'The princess
won't even have time to squeak
when we kidnap 'er!'

'Rat-nap, you mean – ha ha!'
joked the first. 'Just think of the

ransom! All that lovely gold an' silver! Ooh arr!'

Anton shivered at the bottom of the barrel. And then it happened: he sneezed! Ah, AH, CHOO!

All at once, there were Pirats everywhere.

'It's a spy! Grab 'im! Give 'im a taste o' steel!' they shouted.

'No! Take 'im to the cap'n!' cried one. ''E'll know what to do with 'im!'

'We've captured a spy, cap'n! Sneakin' about an' armed to the teeth!' lied one of the crew proudly.

'Well, well, well,' growled Captain Ratfink in a horrible rattle. 'So, the Water Rats is sendin' little 'uman spies now, eh? Well, blast yer breeches! I'll teach you an' yer lily-livered masters a lesson y'll never fergit! Prepare the plan, me lads! Let's 'ave some fun afore we kidnaps the princess. Ooh arr!'

The Pirats sailed the bad ship *Rattlesnake* into the deepest part of the moat.

'You won't get away with this!' cried Anton.

'Ha ha!' laughed Ratfink. 'That's what you think! Y're doomed, me

lad, doomed! Y'hear? Ooh arr! Ha ha! Now jump! Or y'll feel me steel! Ha ha!'

The crew cheered as Anton toppled from the plank, hit the water and began slowly to sink. Down, down, down, he went. Down into the deep blue silence . . .

65

Anton struggled to free himself
but it was useless. Thoughts rushed
through his head: Mum and Dad
will never know what happened to
me . . . They'll . . . Oh!

Suddenly, out of the blue, he saw
two shapes swimming towards him.
Water Rats!

They grabbed Anton and swam
for the shore as fast as their paws
could take them. They pulled the
coughing, spluttering Anton ashore.

'You saved my life,' panted
Anton. 'Just wait till I get my hands

on that Ratfink! But, listen, perhaps I can pay you back for your kindness. You must take me to your king. I need to speak to him at once!'

In the palace of the Water Rats, Anton told his story to the astonished court.

'Oh dear!' cried the king. 'Oh dear! Oh dear, dear, dear! How terrible, how horrible, how, how NASTY! We must lock the doors and hide the princess. Send for Princess Lily, Prime Minister.'

'But, sire,' replied the PM, 'she's out taking her afternoon walk by the . . . moat!'

The king turned pale. The queen fainted. The throne room was silent.

Suddenly the royal nurse burst into the room screaming, 'The princess is kidnapped! The princess is kidnapped!'

'We must save her!' cried Anton. 'Let's get after them.'

'Er, well, yes, I, um, we, that is,' dithered the king, digging furiously in his robes. 'Now, where did I put the key to the armoury? Must sharpen the swords. Er, um, Prime Minister, we do have swords, don't we?'

'Er, well, I, er, that is, I'll have to check the records, Your Majesty,' said the prime minister, his knees knocking like castanets.

'Hurry up!' shouted Anton. 'They'll get away!'

But no one moved.

'We must attack at once with every Water Rat you have!' shrieked Anton.

'Er, well, you see, er, armies take

time,' said the king. 'Er, um, Pirats, you say . . .'

'Will no one come with me?' demanded Anton.

The courtiers shuffled their feet and avoided his eyes.

'I'll come,' said a little rat called Twitcher.

'Good for you!' said Anton. 'Get me some dry clothes and a sword and we'll go on ahead.'

'Jolly good idea,' muttered the king. 'Go on ahead and we'll er, um . . .'

But Anton and Twitcher had
gone.

'Ha ha!' laughed Ratfink. 'That
were the easiest day's work I've
ever done!'

'Let me go,' screamed Princess
Lily. 'Just wait
till my father
hears about
this!'

'Your father,'
cackled Ratfink,
enjoying himself, 'is

as soft as clarts! As weak as water! He's a drip! He couldn't punch his way out of a wet paper bag! Ya ha!'

The other two Pirats were helpless with laughter at their captain's jokes.

'Let me at 'em!' hissed Twitcher.

'No!' said Anton, holding him back. 'We'll have to wait till dark. Maybe by then some of your Water Rats will have joined us.'

Darkness came, but the reinforcements did not.

'Looks like it's up to us,' said Anton. 'Come on, let's go.'

Silently they climbed the mooring ropes of the *Rattlesnake*. They found the princess, tied to the mainmast and fast asleep. (Ratfink, never dreaming the Water Rats would attempt anything so brave as a rescue, had not even bothered to post a guard.)

'This is going to be easy!' whispered Anton to Twitcher.

Anton slashed through the ropes.

Princess Lily woke with a start and, thinking it was the Pirats, screamed, 'Take your hands off me, you smelly sewer rats! You vermin!'

Before Anton could explain, the ship was alive with startled Pirats.

'Quick, Twitcher!' cried Anton. 'Get the princess out of here, I'll hold them for as long as I can!'

'It be a ghost!' yelled the Pirats.

'Ghost or not,' bellowed the captain, "e's no match for Ratfink the Pirat! Let's get 'im!'

And the fight began. The crew cheered as, slowly but surely, Anton, fighting furiously, was forced back and back, until at last he could retreat no further.

'Shiver me whiskers!' laughed Ratfink. 'This 'ere's no ghost: 'e fights like a rat! Ooh arr!' Anton knew it would soon be over. The end was near.

Suddenly from behind the Pirats came a mighty cheer. It came from a hundred furious Water Rats swarming aboard the *Rattlesnake,* screaming and yelling and waving their swords in the air.

Ratfink quickly recovered from his

75

shock. 'Avast, me 'earties,' he cried
to his crew. 'Ha ha! They're only
Water Rats lettin' off a bit o'
steam! They're no match for Pirat
steel.'

But his crew wasn't listening.
They were running for their lives.
Running and jumping over the
side like, well, like rats deserting a
sinking ship!

Ratfink fought bravely but he was
outnumbered a hundred to one.

The clashing and flashing of steel
filled the moonlit night. At last

Ratfink lost his footing and fell with a yell into the moat.

The crew dragged their captain on to the ship's rowing boat and the *Rattlesnake* Pirats lurched off into the night — to the sound of Water-Rat cheers and the rasping voice of Ratfink cursing horribly.

The King of the Water Rats thanked Anton, then Princess Lily kissed him. Anton blushed down to his toes.

'Er, well, er, I, er, had better be going,' said Anton. 'My family will be ever so worried about me.'

To the thunderous applause of the Water Rats, Anton said farewell to Twitcher and slid down the mooring ropes to the bank.

The warm lights of the castle welcomed our hero home.

As he walked across the drawbridge, Anton B. Stanton shouted into the night, 'Shiver me timbers, but fightin' Pirats makes a fellow hungry. Ooh arr!'

Beaky McCreaky, Parrot of the High Seas

Fiona Dunbar

So I'm sitting on my perch in
Captain Skunk's cabin, and there's
Midshipman Vole scraping fungus
off the ceiling with his knife.

The scritching sound wakes
Skunk (he's been snoozing after his

morning rum). 'What's that noise?' he barks.

'Oh, nothing, Cap'n,' says Vole. 'I were only scrapin' the ceiling, sir, cos I'm missin' my sweetheart back 'ome something awful, see.'

Skunk swivels his solitary eye at Vole. 'Ye blazin' bilge rat, what the jiggerin' gibbets has the one got to do with the other?'

'Well, Cap'n,' says Vole, 'I's written her a letter, see, and now I needs some ceiling wax to seal it up with.'

Skunk slams his fist on the table. 'Ye bloomin' idiot! The *ceiling* ain't where *sealing* wax comes from! Anyhow, we don't got no sealing wax on board this ship, Vole. Any idea why?'

Vole scrunches his eyes tight shut and thinks hard. 'Ur, no, Cap'n.'

'Because the *postman* don't come around these parts too often!' bellows Skunk. The timbers creak and the waves lash against the window.

Vole hangs his head and stares

sadly at his letter. 'Oh yeah, I s'pose not.'

Now, being the only one with any brains around here, I give a loud 'SQUAWK!' and flap my wings, because, of course, I've worked out that *I* could deliver the letter.

And Skunk, taking my cue, says, 'But you're in luck, Vole. We've got airmail – courtesy of Beaky here!'

'Oh! Right!' says Vole, beaming from ear to ear and showing all two teeth.

82

Off I fly with the letter clamped
in my beak. I don't deliver it, of
course, because Vole
hasn't addressed it;
he's forgotten he
can't write.
All he's put
are squiggles
and love hearts. But he
believes his message has been sent,
so he's happy.

Honestly, it's like this all the time.
The captain's not so dumb, but he's
constantly sozzled. He was sozzled

when he hired his crew, which is why they've got about as much brains between them as a barrel of maggoty malt-grain. If you thought it was *pirates* that ruled the High Seas, well, you're wrong. It's us parrots.

So when I come back from feeding Vole's letter to the sharks, I find the ship going around in circles, because they can't navigate without me. The twins, Ugg and Ogg, are at the helm, and Ogg's saying, 'We got to keep heading to starboard, cos land's that way, and we didn't get there yet.' And Ugg's scratching his nit-infested head. 'I don't know,' he says. 'Either the sun's swinging from one side o' the sky to t'other today, or, or—'

'Squawk!' I say, and perch in front of them. Uttering 'port!' and 'starboard!' from time to time, I set us back on course. I'm not one to blow my own trumpet, but what *would* they do without me?

The wind is getting up now, and it starts to rain. Time for me to

retreat to my cage. Which is fine,
until the storm builds, making the
cage swing back and forth like a
church bell, and slamming the door
shut. Soon I'm sick as a parrot,
hiding in the corner under my
wing. At last, Captain Skunk
comes in to top
up his rum flask
and lets me out.

'Cap'n!'
yells Vole,
stumbling into
the room.

'There's ever so much water about!'

'Well of course there is!' splutters Skunk. 'It's a *storm*, ye blitherin' rodent-brain!'

'Oh, aye, Cap'n, right . . . so it is,' nods Vole happily. He turns to leave. 'Well, I'll be off then, Cap'n. Gonna take a nice swim down below.'

The captain coughs loudly. 'Swim?! You mean the water's *in the ship*?'

'Why, yes, sir,' says Vole, his smile dropping instantly.

Skunk thunders down into the bowels of the ship, and Vole and I follow.

Slosh, slosh: we're filling up rapidly. 'Let's chuck this stuff overboard, it's weighin' us down,' says the captain, picking up a grand oak chair. Vole does likewise, and they lug the furniture up to the deck. I fly on ahead, to check on what the other men are doing. Just as well: Ugg and Ogg are about to throw over the last of the rum kegs.

Knowing how Captain Skunk would feel about this, I squawk loudly and fly at Ugg's head. He drops his end of the keg and it lands on his foot. 'Ow!' he yells.

'Good job, Beaky,' says the Captain, gasping with relief when he arrives. 'We've got to keep hold of that! Er, for *emergencies*, y'understand.'

'Oh, right,' says Ogg. 'Cos we wasn't sure what to get rid of next, what with all o' them sacks we already done thrown overboard . . .'

Skunk's eye swivels in its socket. 'Sacks? Did you say *sacks*?'

'Why, yes,' says Ogg. 'Real heavy, them was. But we's *strong*, Cap'n!' He proudly shows off his bulging biceps. 'We got rid o' every last one!'

The captain lunges forward and pulls out his pistol. 'Remember the time you tried to pierce your ear by shooting a hole through it, Ogg, and blasted off your right cheek?'

Ogg scratches what remains of the right side of his ghastly face. 'Aye, Cap'n.'

90

Skunk thrusts his sweaty face at Ogg. 'Well how about we make the OTHER side MATCH?!'

'Ooh no, Cap'n!' pleads Ogg, his knees quaking. 'It hurt somethin' awful!'

'Not 'alf as much as your BELLY'S going to hurt when it's had nothing inside it for fourteen days!' yells the captain. 'You just threw over our whole grain store, yer pair of gibberin' apes! We've nothing left to eat.'

'Uh-oh.'

Five Days Later

This is one predicament even I can't get us out of. With no food to soak up the rum, the drunken captain now sleeps all day long. The other pirates have taken to keeping me cooped up in my cage and looking at me in a funny way.

Ugg presses his bulbous nose up against the bars. 'I'm *starvin'*,' he groans.

'Yur, so am I,' says Ogg. The stench of his breath almost makes me keel over. 'That were the last rat we et yesterday, and them candles 'as given me gut-rot.' He pokes his cutlass through the bars of my cage. 'Now, a nice dish o' *roast parrot*; that would go down a treat.'

'Squaawwwk!' I respond, flapping away from the blade.

Vole looks troubled. 'No, not our Beaky! He don't deserve that. Besides, how would we manage without 'im?'

'Well . . .' says Ugg, thoughtfully

rubbing his stubbly chin. 'All right — we won't eat 'im . . . *just* yet.'

Another day passes. The captain snores through everything. The pirates have eaten all my nuts and seeds, and now they're eyeing me up again. 'Can't leave it any longer, 'e'll only get all scrawny,' says Ugg. 'Let's have 'im now, while 'e's nice and plump. Come on, Ogg; let's go tell Cook to get the oven on.'

My fate is sealed. Even my old

pal Vole has an evil glint in his eye.
I'm dead meat.

But then, of course, I have an
idea.

'Love letter!' I squawk through
the bars of my cage.

'What?' says Vole.

'Love letter!' I repeat.

Vole clutches his belly. 'A love
letter . . . yes! If I die o' starvation
out here, I will never see my
beloved again. You're right, Beaky,
I must write her one last letter!'

So he starts filling a page with

squiggles and love hearts, and, when he's done, sniffing back the tears, he lets me out of the cage and gives me the letter to deliver. By the time he realizes his mistake it's too late; I'm away.

I'm flapping merrily skyward, free as a bird at last, when I reflect that in spite of everything, I am rather fond of poor old Vole. His heart's in the right place: I mean, it wasn't *his* idea to eat me. And even Ogg was only trying to survive. So when at last I get to an island, I break off a palm frond and wing it back to the ship (which is circling slowly in exactly the same spot where I left it).

The starving crew go berserk. 'Hurray for Beaky!' they cheer, because even that bunch of boneheads realizes that the palm frond means land. I guide them back to the island, which has pure white sand, blue sky, lush vegetation; it's a paradise. The pirates practically swoon as they gaze hungrily at the mangoes, coconuts, dates, fresh fish and turtles. My work here is done, I reflect proudly, until my thoughts are interrupted by a loud 'Ow!'.

I look round and catch sight of Ogg trying to crack open a coconut with his forehead. 'Me poor 'ed!'

Hmm. On second thoughts, perhaps I'll stick around a little longer . . .

The Treasure of Shark's Tooth Island

David Harmer

Ben Carver, nine years old and
terrified, skidded and slipped on
the stones along the shoreline. He
was running fast, but behind him
he could hear the thump of heavy
sea-boots. Mad Mason and his crew

of pirates were gaining on him.
He stopped, panting for breath,
fear and sweat making him shiver.
He had nowhere to hide. The
island was a long, thin slab of rock
battered by churning seas, a clump
of weather-beaten trees clinging to
its centre. That was the only shelter.
Here on the beach, they'd find him
in a moment.

He started to run again, feeling
the key swing on its leather strap
around his neck, a hard fist of
iron that banged and bruised him.

He was going to die here on this miserable island, all for the key his father had given him two years before. Once Mad Mason got hold of it, there would be no further need of the young cabin boy.

Ben stopped, shaking his head, swallowing a gulp of air. Then, as there was nothing else to do, he turned to run once more. Straight away he banged into something extremely solid. He found himself sitting down, dazed, the sea soaking his breeches. Somebody grunted and a giant hand grabbed him by the shoulder and hauled him skywards. 'So now we meet, Master Carver,' said the huge man. 'Seems you've run into Jago at last.'

Ben found himself looking into the coldest eyes he had ever seen,

as bleak as the sea in winter. The eyes were framed by long black hair, salted with grey, rolling down to the man's shoulders. A cruel scar stretched from the edge of his left eyebrow down to his chin. Big hoops of gold swung from his ears and he bristled with knives, pistols and a long curved cutlass.

'Where is it, lad, eh? Tell me where it is.'

He twisted Ben upside down, so that his face was scraped by the sharp stones of the beach.

'I-I-I'm not scared of you,' stuttered the boy. 'Tha-tha-that I am not.'

The next moment, Ben was whirled so fiercely that the blood pounded in his ears and he felt dizzy and sick.

'Well you should be scared, shipmate,' growled the man. 'For I am Captain Sparke of the pirate ship *Firebird*. And I tell you, boy, everyone I meet is frightened of me.'

Ben's stomach turned over. He'd

heard too many dreadful stories about this bloodthirsty buccaneer not to feel real panic sweep through him.

'Here's someone else who ain't scared of you,' growled a new voice, 'and my pistol is about to blow your brains out.'

Another pirate appeared from the darkness, with ten of his crew, each pointing a weapon at the large, grinning face.

'Mad Mason,' said Jago Sparke, dumping the boy like a sack of flour. 'Well, well. Perhaps before you does that, you'd like to meet my lads, eh? The ones with the muskets pointing at your heads.'

'You're lying, scurvy dog,' said Mason. He cocked his pistol and took steady aim.

In the same instant, the muzzle of a musket was rammed into his ear. 'Oh, just you try it, my lad,' whispered Abel Monkshood, first mate of the *Firebird,* as Mason's sneer of triumph dissolved into a whimper of fear.

'Throw down your weapons,' ordered Jago Sparke as twenty more of his crew materialized from the darkness. 'The lot of them. Now.'

Instantly a pile of cutlasses, knives, pistols and wooden cudgels clattered on to the rocky beach.

'Right, shipmate,' said Sparke to the boy, who by now had struggled to his feet, shaken and scratched. 'I'll take it now, if you please.' Fixing Ben with an icy stare, he deftly cut the key free from its moorings.

108

'That's mine!' shouted Mad Mason. He leaped forward, but Sparke's massive fist shot out and Mason slumped to the ground, holding his jaw and moaning.

The moon sprang out from behind the clouds and the beach was suddenly turned silver, grey and white. Ben felt despair, then anger, overwhelm him.

He ran at his tormentor. 'Robber! Thief! My father gave me that key.'

'Enough!' roared Sparke. 'Your own father was a pirate, as well you know. Cut-Throat Carver. Sailed with me and Mason here more than thirty years ago. Some time or another he buried his treasure on this island. We've been following you and Mason for weeks now. So enough of all this blubbering and wailing. Mr Monkshood, take one of the lads here and go and find the chest. It'll be on the sand, back there, where Mason and his men dug it up.'

Beckoning a crew member to join him, Abel Monkshood began to walk towards the treasure. Ben saw that he was a mountain of a man, his shaven head tattooed with a swarm of purple snakes. The pirate caught Ben's stare and turned to look at him.

'Now then, shaver,' he said softly, his eyes glowing, 'mind these vipers don't bite you, eh?' With that he was gone, his laughter booming through the night.

'Right,' continued Jago Sparke, 'let's have these bilge rats tied up, all tight and secure.'

A dozen men set to work. Before long, Mad Mason and his crew looked less like sinister pirates and more like bundles of thick ship's rope.

A few moments later, Abel Monkshood and his companion returned, carrying a large sea chest between them. Ben saw how heavy it was; even the enormous first mate was straining under its weight. They set it down and it gleamed in the bright moonlight.

Sparke whistled. 'No wonder your

friend Mason here needed your key, boy. A pistol shot would have ruined this wonderful thing forever.'

The chest was covered entirely in gems and pearls, looking like a rare treasure from a king's palace. Sparke knelt down beside it and rubbed his hands over the curved lid.

'Look at this, Mason,' he laughed. 'At last! Carver's treasure. After all these years, eh?'

Mason struggled in his bonds. 'I'll have my revenge, Sparke, and when I do . . .'

Before he knew it, the other man had grabbed his tongue and a knife flickered.

'You'll do what, shipmate?' whispered Sparke, the moon making the blade ripple and dance. 'Well? With no tongue?'

Mason gurgled, sweat running down his face.

Jago Sparke stared at him, hard, and then released his grip.

'Keep your tongue this time, Mason,' he said, 'but keep your distance too.' He looked at the

boy. 'Let's open her up, eh, Ben?
See what great treasure Cut-Throat
Carver left you.'

Kneeling, he carefully slid the
key into the lock and turned it.
There was a soft clunk as the
chest opened. Ben held his breath.
Everything went quiet. It seemed
that all the men on that beach,
rough and violent though they
were, felt as excited as children at
Christmas time.

Jago Sparke looked into the chest
for several moments. Then, he flung

back his head and a huge gust of laughter bellowed out.

'Nothing! Full of stones. And this. A piece of painted canvas. Here, boy! Take a look. It's you.'

Trembling, Ben stepped over and

BEN, MY GREATEST TREASURE

took the roll of cloth. He gasped. It was indeed a painting of him, aged four or five. Underneath was written in a rough hand, 'Ben, my greatest treasure.'

'And these pearls and gems stuck on like limpets?' continued Sparke. 'Worthless! Paste and glass, that's all. Your father certainly fooled us.'

The pirate got to his feet and began signalling his men back towards their longboat. He turned to Ben.

'So, shipmate, what are we going

to do with you?' He looked at Mad
Mason and his crew. 'You can't
stay here with this miserable bunch,
can you? Why not come along with
old Jago? Live the pirate life like
your old dad used to, roaming the
oceans without a care. Who knows,
one day they might sing of Cut-
Throat *Ben* Carver.'

'Don't listen to him, boy,' hissed
Mad Mason. 'Cut me free.'

The same Mad Mason who
would have left him there for dead.

Ben shook his head, as the pirate,

struggling furiously, overbalanced and tumbled head first into a puddle of stagnant sea-water.

The boy laughed and, clutching his precious painting, ran off into the night after his new captain: Jago Sparke of the bold ship *Firebird*.

Captain Whiskers and the Fishy Tail

Anna Wilson

Fidget was miserable. He had always dreamed of sailing the stormy seas and performing heroic deeds of derring-do. With this in mind, he had landed himself a job as a cabin boy for a crew of pirates on the *Slinky Susan*. Dastardly Des, the quartermaster of the ship, had persuaded Fidget to join him and his gang, promising a life of adventure on the high seas. But the most adventure Fidget got once he was on board was to wash the pirates' socks, which in itself required a fair amount of heroism. On top of that, Dastardly Des made his life hell.

Every morning Des beat him, shouted at him and then beat him again for good measure, before throwing him on deck and roaring,

'Swab them boards till yer can see yer ugly face in them, boy!'

Fidget always thought it was a bit hypocritical to call *him* ugly. But then, they didn't have mirrors on board, so Dastardly Des had never seen his own warty, hairy mug.

Fidget was also rather perplexed as to why Des was so keen on keeping the decks clean, when his own personal hygiene left so much to be desired. All the pirates were a hairy, smelly, belching, filthy, scurvy-ridden bunch of louts, and

Fidget was desperate to think of a plan to escape from them.

One morning, very much like the last, Fidget finished swabbing the upper deck and stared sadly out to sea. 'I wish someone would come and take me away from all this,' he said to himself.

Luckily Fidget did have a couple of friends on board with whom to share his woes. One was none other than good Captain Whiskers. Whiskers was a suave, debonair sort of chap. He wore a shiny black

coat and was always well groomed.
Now, you may think that being
friends with the captain would have
made Fidget's life on the ship much
more tolerable, but unfortunately
the crew didn't pay much heed to
Captain Whiskers — who spent most
of his days snoozing.

Fidget climbed below decks to
put away his mop and bucket
and almost tripped over Captain
Whiskers, who was, guess what,
taking a nap at the bottom of the
steps. He woke with a yawn and

stretched his limbs luxuriously. He gave his wooden leg a little shake. Then he daintily adjusted his white eyepatch and looked up cautiously to see who had disturbed his rest. Captain Whiskers did everything cautiously – he never knew when an enemy might be about to pounce.

'Oh, it's you,' he purred, taking in the sorry figure of the skinny cabin boy. 'Be more careful, can't you? I was having a lovely dream of fried kippers and . . .'

'Don't!' moaned Fidget. 'I've eaten nothing but weevils for days. Oh, Captain, I've had enough. I want to go home! Can you help me?'

'It would be a shame to lose you,' Whiskers pondered. 'You're the only member of the crew with whom one can have a decent conversation without being burped at. Still, I suppose I'm being selfish. Let's think . . .'

Whiskers sat up, preened his shiny black coat, lifted his bad leg in the air and swiftly twisted round to lick his bottom.

Yes, Captain Whiskers was a cat – a ship's cat. Ever since he was a cute and cuddly kitten he had sailed the Seven Seas, making full use of his six senses and nimbly avoiding losing any of his nine lives. The secret of his success? His personal motto: 'Wash before you think, and think before you act.' He only wished the pirates would do the same.

When he'd finished washing, the

captain announced his plan. 'I think
we'll have to create a diversion to
allow you to slip away unnoticed.'

Fidget sighed heavily. 'And how
am I going to "slip away", as you
put it, when we're in the middle of
the ocean? I can't swim, and I don't

fancy slipping down to Davy Jones's
locker, thanks very much.'

'All right,' said Whiskers, a bit
put out. '*You* think of something
then.'

At that moment, the second of
Fidget's friends, Pablo Pesos, joined
them. He was a large scarlet and
emerald South American parrot
with feathers like a firework and
a voice to match. 'Hey, *gringos*!'
shouted Pablo. 'I have-a ze Great
News!'

'Shhh! Keep your beak shut,'

hissed Captain Whiskers. 'We're trying to plot Fidget's escape.'

'Escape? You no wanna escape! Not when you hear ze Great News!' squawked the parrot.

'Spit it out then,' said Whiskers wearily.

'Spit what out? I no have nothing in-a my beak!' Pablo looked confused.

'GET ON WITH IT!' yelled the cat.

'Okey-dokey. No need-a to shout,' huffed the parrot. 'So, I

was up in my crow's-nest – hey, why you always call it "crow's-nest" when I am a parrot?' He was getting sidetracked.

'Listen, birdbrain,' began Whiskers, eyeing the parrot dangerously.

'OK! OK! I tell you ze Great News – there is beeeg feeeeesh on starboard side! Come look!'

Whiskers's ears pricked up at the mention of fish. Like Fidget, he had not eaten a decent meal for days. He turned to the cabin boy. 'How are you with a fishing net?' he asked.

Fidget sighed. 'So much for helping me escape,' he said.

The cat washed one paw slowly and then said, 'You'll need a good meal inside you if you've got any chance of outpacing our hairy pirate friends . . . and if you get me and Pablo a tasty morsel, I'm sure we'll be in a better position to help you.'

Fidget smiled. 'You are very cunning, Captain,' he said. 'All

right — keep an eye out for trouble
while I catch your precious fish for
you.'

Fidget crept up to the top deck
with an armful of fishing net,
looking furtively over his shoulder
in case a pirate jumped out at him.
He need not have worried though,
for at that moment Dastardly Des
and the rest of the crew were
below decks, swilling their body-
weight in grog and singing rude
songs very loudly, so they did not
hear him.

Fidget peeped over the starboard side of the ship.

'Well, splice the mainbrace and shiver me timbers!' he cried. 'Pablo's right – look at that!'

Whiskers jumped up on to the rail and caught sight of a huge rainbow-coloured tail ploughing through the waves.

He whistled slowly. 'That, my friend, is a beauty, and no mistake,' he said, licking his lips in anticipation. 'What are you waiting for? Heave-ho, Fidget!' he cried.

The cabin boy bailed the net over the edge and dragged it slowly through the water. Whiskers balanced daintily on the rail, looking down at the sea, and Pablo hovered in the air above them, shouting instructions:

'Left a leetle bit — right a leetle bit — nearly got him!'

Suddenly Fidget felt the net tug sharply and he nearly fell overboard.

'Quick, Pablo! Grab the net in your beak and help me pull,' Fidget ordered.

135

Whiskers jumped down on to the deck just in time as the net was tugged in complete with its writhing, wriggling catch.

It was then that the friends saw what they had captured – and it wasn't a fish.

'Honestly, boys! Can't a girl have a little swim without being hauled out of the water?' the creature whined.

Fidget was speechless. 'You're a – a – a –' he stammered.

The creature batted its extremely

long eyelashes at him and simpered,
'A mermaid! Never thought you'd
see one of those, did you?'

Whiskers was annoyed. 'Great.

We're hallucinating. This is what happens when you don't eat for days. This really takes the biscuit,' he muttered.

Pablo was confused again. 'Beeskit? Beeskit? Who hhhhas taken ze beeskit? We are all starving around hhhhhere already, and now someone hhhhhas taken the beeskit! I will kill hhhhhim, the thief!' screeched the demented bird.

'Oh shut up,' hissed the captain. 'Help me deal with this fish, won't you?'

'Who are you calling a fish?'
asked the mermaid indignantly.
'I may have the tail of a fish,
but I have the body of a princess.
And, what's more, I have magical
powers, so I'd be careful what you
say!'

'You're pulling my leg,' said
Whiskers scathingly.

'How dare you – that's a
tail-ist remark!' cried the mermaid,
struggling to get free of the net.

'Believe me, Fidget,' said
Whiskers, 'she is not real. Mermaids

don't exist. This looks distinctly fishy
to me—'

'Wait a minute!' interrupted
Fidget. He turned to the mermaid.
'Did you say you had magical
powers?' he asked. He didn't care
if she was an illusion brought on
by starvation. He was desperate.
'I could really do with saving.
I've been on this ship for months
working for a lousy bunch of pirates
and—'

'Who you callin' lousy?' bellowed
a voice from across the deck. It was

140

Dastardly Des, the quartermaster. He had overdone the grog a bit and was looking distinctly green about the gills. 'I hope you're goin' to take that lady-fish down to the galley and gut it, boy!' he roared. 'Me and my mates are starvin'! You can do us all a fry-up.' He licked his hairy chops and belched satisfyingly, the green tinge disappearing from his face at the thought of a fish supper.

'I will not!' cried Fidget. 'This is no lady-fish – she is a beautiful mermaid. And she doesn't deserve to be cooked and eaten by the likes of you lot. Come on,' he said, turning to the mermaid. 'Back you go!'

And before the astonished eyes of the smelly pirate, Fidget helped the mermaid out of the net and overboard into the sea.

'Thank you, kind sir!' she cried, flicking her silky locks over her shoulder. 'Now, one kind turn deserves another, so hop on my tail and I'll take you wherever you want to go.'

Fidget hesitated. 'What about Whiskers here – and Pablo?' he asked. 'I can't leave them with those cruel pirates.'

The mermaid glanced up at Dastardly Des, who was approaching the group, his cutlass glinting in the sunlight. Then she looked at Fidget and saw how dearly he wanted to save his friends.

She decided to forgive the cat's earlier insults and said, 'All right – but no nibbling at my tail, moggy!'

Whiskers was about to make

a cutting remark, but then took one look at the stinky pirate and decided he too had had enough of life on the *Slinky Susan*. He leaped into the air before the pirate could catch him (which was not difficult, as Des only had one hand) and landed on the mermaid's tail, closely followed by Fidget.

'So where to, chaps?' she asked.

'Anywhere, so long as it's far away from that lot,' Fidget replied, looking nervously over his shoulder at the quartermaster.

'Hey! I a-coming a-too,' cried
Pablo, flying alongside his friends.
'I have enough of these stinky,
dcesgusting men! I show you
the way to my old home in the
rainforest – ees BEAUTIFUL place.'

Fidget laughed. 'Sounds good
to me!' The mermaid plunged
through the waves, following Pablo,
and Fidget cried out, 'Bye-bye,
Dastardly Des! Give my love to the
crew. And don't worry about your
supper – there are plenty more fish
in the sea.'

The pirate howled and waved his cutlass in the air, but for once there was nothing he could do. The friends were already far from the ship, swimming out into the bright blue yonder.

'Thanks, Mermaid,' said Fidget, patting her scales. 'And thanks, Pablo, for spotting her!'

The parrot squawked happily from the skies.

'And thank you, Captain, for coming with me,' Fidget added. 'You really are the cat's whiskers.'

Spilt Milk

Philip Ardagh

'I've had an idea,' said Snitch.

'An idea?' asked the first mate.

'An idea,' nodded Snitch.

'What about?' asked the first mate.

'About the flag,' said Snitch.

'Oh, goodie!' said Captain Splat,

147

looking up from his large plate of salt beef and weevils. (The weevils weren't a part of the recipe. They lived with the beef in the barrels of salt so, nine times out of ten – or ten times out of eleven, if you were greedy – you got weevils in your beef.) 'Do tell!'

'We're pirates, right?' said Snitch.

'Right!' agreed Captain Splat and his first mate.

'And what's our greatest weapon?'

'My cutlass?' the captain suggested,

waving his knife and fork around in a somewhat dangerous manner.

The first mate frowned. 'That great big cannon on the starboard side?' he asked a little uncertainly. He wasn't a big fan of quizzes.

'There's a cannon on my sideboard?' asked Captain Splat, looking around his cabin in surprise. (Although the captain's cabin was by far the biggest on the ship, it was rather cramped.) He accidentally jabbed the poor first mate in the face with his elbow.

'I said starboard side, Captain, not *sideboard*,' said the first mate, nursing his nose. Blood dripped from the end of it. He looked less than pleased.

'Starboard?' asked the captain, already shovelling in another mouthful of salt beef (and weevils).

'It's on the opposite side to the port,' said Snitch.

'But we're not in port,' said Splat. He looked a trifle confused.

Snitch sighed. Conversations with the captain were always a little like this. They seemed to go round and round in circles, in much the same way that the *Lightning Strike* went round and round in circles whenever Captain Splat chose to steer.

'One side of the ship is called the port side and the other is the starboard side, remember, Captain? It's like left and right. Port and starboard.'

'Aha!' nodded Splat, whose mind was already on something else. He was probably thinking about fresh vegetables. You didn't get many of them when you were in the middle of a sea voyage.

'The flag, Snitch,' said the first mate. 'You were about to tell us your idea for the flag.'

'Oh yes,' agreed Snitch, glad to be getting back to the matter in hand. 'A pirate's greatest weapon is fear.'

Captain Splat struggled to his feet to the sound of crashing plates. 'I'm not afraid of anyone!' he roared. He was an impressive sight with the corner of the tablecloth

tucked into the neck of his shirt as a giant napkin. It was covered in splodges and splats. (I wonder if that's where he got his name from?)

'Of course you're not, Captain,' said Snitch. 'That's exactly my point! At the very mention of the word PIRATE, God-fearing seafaring folk start a-trembling.'

The captain puffed his chest out with pride. His face then broke into a beautiful smile, revealing one of the finest sets of rotting black teeth ever to have graced the face of one

who'd sailed six of the Seven Seas.
(He never could find the seventh.
Someone had sold him a map with
rather too many blanks and 'There
Be Dragons', and too little detail.)

'So, we need to invent a pirate
flag which will add to that fear the
moment we run it up the mast!' said
Snitch triumphantly.

'Genius!' said the captain, sitting
back down again, and picking bits
of food from his enormous beard,
which he proceeded to pop into his
mouth.

'What about one with a rat?' suggested the first mate. 'Most sailors hate rats.'

'Or a great big hairy spider?' said Captain Splat. 'I've never liked spiders . . . Not that I've ever been *afraid* of them,' he quickly added.

'I know! I know!' cried the first mate. His voice had gone all squeaky with excitement. 'How about a leak? Sailors are afraid of leaks!'

'Leeks?' The captain frowned. 'Why should anyone be afraid of a vegetable?' (Half his mind was still on matters foody.)

'Leaks as in water-gushing-through-a-hole-in-the-bottom-of-the-ship leaks,' said the first mate. 'Leaks as in abandon-ship-we're-sinking leaks.'

'That might be quite difficult to draw on a flag,' said Snitch cautiously. He was being cautious because he didn't want to upset the first mate, who – after Captain Splat himself – was the most important person on board the

Lightning Strike. When the first mate got upset he threatened the crew with the 'cat-o'-nine-tails'. (Snitch had never actually seen the cat-o'-nine-tails but, being more of a dog person than a cat person, imagined that it must be rather a frightening beast requiring an extra-large litter tray.) 'It's a truly splendid idea . . . but someone might mistake a picture of a leak for a spout from a whale—'

'Or an ornamental fountain!' said the captain with a guffaw. 'But, to

158

more immediate matters, I'm ready for my pudding now!' He produced a large, and somewhat dented, spoon from an inside pocket of his purple crushed-velvet frock coat.

The first mate threw open the door on to the deck and called out, 'Bring the captain's pudding!'

'What I was thinking,' Snitch went on, 'was of having a black flag—'

'Excellent!' said the captain. 'It won't show the dirt much. That'll please Tubs. Less washing.' Tubs

was in charge of all laundry aboard
the *Lightning Streak*. She pretended
to be a very large man, and
everyone else on board pretended
they thought that she *was* a very
large man, but everyone knew that

she was really a very large woman.
She pretended to be a very large
man because she didn't think that
women pirates were allowed . . .
which was strange, because Bosun
Brenda, Gunner Glenda and
Fairly-Able-Seaman Fiona were
all women, and nobody seemed
to mind. (Perhaps it was because
they were so willing to share their
earrings. There are few things
pirates like more than gold earrings
except, of course, buried treasure.)

'A black flag sounds pretty boring

to me,' said the first mate without thinking. His words were slightly muffled, because he'd removed his pirate neckerchief and was holding it up against his bleeding nose.

'The black's just the background,' Snitch explained.

'And a very good choice of background too,' commented the captain. 'It'll remind people of death and funerals, which is just what we want them to be thinking about before we attack . . . Now, where's my pudding got to?'

The first mate threw open the door again. 'Where's the captain's pudding?' he demanded. There was a sudden burst of activity, with pirates dashing hither and thither (via here and there) across the decks in an effort to get the captain his food as soon as possible. A still-hungry captain would be an unhappy captain and an unhappy captain would soon mean an unhappy ship. The first mate would make sure of that.

Snitch, meanwhile, was laying his

prototype pirate flag on the table: two white crossed cutlasses on a background as black as midnight. (A particularly dark midnight, with no moon or stars.)

Captain Splat looked at it. The first mate turned and looked at it. The first mate didn't want to say anything until he knew what the captain thought. If the captain liked it, *he'd* like it. If the captain thought it was a silly idea, *he'd* think it was a silly idea. That way he avoided (a) being made to walk the plank, and (b) losing the position of first mate.

Splat hmmmmmed. 'Hmmmmmm,' he said.

So the first mate hmmmmmed. 'Hmmmmmm,' he said.

At that moment, the door flew open and Roger the cabin boy hurried in with a tray. On it was a bowl containing a single hard-tack biscuit floating in a sea of goat's milk. (The pirates had recently boarded a galleon and stolen a goat belonging to the Queen of Spain's

165

cousin, Isabella.) 'Your pudding,
Captain,' said the boy.

'Goody!' said Captain Splat,
spoon at the ready.

Just as the cabin boy passed the
bowl across the table, the *Lightning
Strike* hit a few bumps in the ocean
– waves, I think they're called –
and some of the goat's milk slopped
on to Snitch's flag.

Roger the cabin boy froze with
fear. How would the captain react?
Snitch looked down at his flag
in horror. The first mate held his

breath, wondering whether he'd need to administer the cat-o'-nine-tails.

Captain Splat smiled. 'That's much better,' he said, scrutinizing the flag, now modified with a big white splodge above the crossed swords. 'It looks a bit like a skull . . . and there's nothing more frightening than a skull now, is there?'

'No, Captain,' said Snitch, the first mate and the cabin boy.

The captain picked up his fork

and dipped it into the milk, using it like a paintbrush. 'There,' he said, admiring his handiwork. 'The crossed cutlasses work better as crossed bones . . . A skull and crossbones! The ideal pirate flag. I like it! And, what's more, I think we should name it after the one who created it,' he announced.

Snitch glowed with pride.

'An excellent idea, Captain,' said the first mate. 'Most fitting.' Personally, he thought that 'Snitch' was a silly name for a flag – he thought it was a silly name for a *person* too, if truth be told – but, once again, he knew better than to express an opinion.

Captain Splat ran the fork across the bottom of milk-splodge skull, creating a splendid grin. He looked up at the relieved cabin boy. 'I shall call it the Jolly Roger,' he said. 'Now, get me some tea! I want tea!'

Snitch sighed another sigh, then went back to his cabin.

Jolly Roger *n.* the pirate flag with a white skull and crossbones on a black background – eighteenth century: *origin unknown*

170

Dame Peggie Slops and her Haunted Wooden Leg

Ian Billings

This was the Cluttered Plughole
– and it lived up to its name. It
was a tatty tavern that was home
from home to a fearsome fleet of
plucky pirates. All shapes and sizes

were washed up in the Cluttered Plughole: pirates from across the globe, pirates from across the street, each with a salty tale to tell of adventures at sea.

Mr Blackbarrel, the musician, was hunched over the grotty grand piano and his spindly fingers poked the battered keys like tongs poking a fire. As he poked out a sea shanty, snatches of conversations could be heard.

'Of course, my head was stuck in the cannon for a week . . .'

'Then I grabbed him by the ears and flung him overboard . . .'

'I didn't know he had a glass eye until it came out in conversation . . .'

'Cheese and onion crisps, please!'

The last sound came from a voice that belonged to a mouth that was owned by a face which had at one time been very familiar in these parts.

'Dame Peggie Slops!' croaked Mr Click, the barman, unable to believe what he was seeing. A few heads turned as he croaked his croak.

'Dame Peggie Slops!' he cried.

173

'There she blows! One of the finest pirates ever to nick a clipper out of Portsmouth. Tales of the derring-do she's dared do are part of the folklore hereabouts!'

Mr Blackbarrel battered a hearty tune from the piano in celebration as the barman filled a frothy tankard for their star guest. He leaned across the wet bar and said, 'So, Dame Peggie, what brings you back?'

Dame Peggie Slops was a sprightly pirate. Her long white hair tressed down her back and she had the complexion of someone half her age. She was seventy-two and still had all her own teeth – in a jar by her bed. She slipped the crisps from the barman's grasp and her twinkling eyes gave him a naughty wink as she slid away.

The barman sighed as she went, but then he noticed Dame Peggie was limping and using a stick. She never used to limp, he thought as he turned to the next customer.

In a quiet corner of the tavern sat

175

a small man with a hat too large for his head and a smile too wide for his face. The smile widened as Dame Peggie limped towards him.

Was this the man she was looking for?

'Would you like a cheese and onion crisp?' she asked, opening the packet and offering its contents. This was a pre-arranged code — if he gave the correct answer she would know he was the man.

'Thank you,' he said, 'but I only eat salt and vinegar.'

Dame Peggie crunched the packet, threw it aside and slid into the seat next to him. That was the correct answer. 'Doctor Residue?' she asked.

The man lifted his hat and almost took off his fake wig too.

'The same!' he said, and the smile slithered across his face. 'So you'd like a wooden leg, would you?'

Dame Peggie hushed him and explained in a low voice, 'I have tangled with the vilest villains afloat and have never had a scar, a bruise or even a graze! But three months

177

ago I encountered a pack of the most vicious penguins you could imagine and, well –' she grimaced at the memory – 'I will not go into too much detail, but where I once had two legs I now only have one.'

Doctor Residue scanned the chattering masses of the tavern and then bent down under the table. He re-emerged clutching a large leather suitcase with big brass clasps, which, like his face, had not been cleaned for a very long time. He clicked the clasps and the lid popped open.

He turned the case just enough for Dame Peggie to see its contents without revealing them to the pub.

The old sea-saltress gasped. Inside the suitcase, nestling amongst plush red velvet, were five wooden legs.

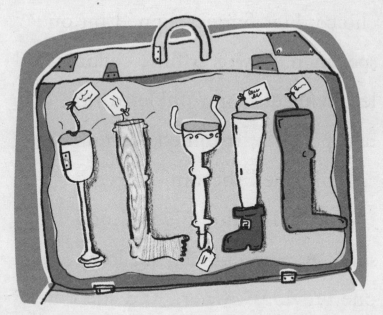

'This is just what I need,' whispered Dame Peggie.

'But which will you choose?' asked the doctor.

She ran her hand over the legs and slowly began making her choice. Her finger stopped on one specimen. It was a fine, cedar-wood leg, with a strong ankle, a firm calf and perfectly trimmed toenails.

'This one!' she announced.

Doctor Residue giggled and said, 'A wise choice, my lady, only one previous owner. And she only used it for going to the shops on a Sunday.'

He slipped the leg from the case, wrapped it in brown paper and handed it over.

Dame Peggie hid it in the folds of her dress and smiled at the doctor.

'And my money?' he asked.

Dame Peggie produced a bag of gold coins from another fold and slid it across the table. They nodded at each other and both disappeared into the crowd.

The deed was done, the

181

agreement was sealed and the story had begun.

Dame Peggie scurried away into the darkest darkness of the night. Clutched under her grateful arm was the leg she had yearned for. That night she would practise her foxtrot, her tango and her cha-cha like there was no tomorrow. But there was a tomorrow and it would be the day of the Pirate Ball. Dame Peggie was determined to be the finest dancer there — and with her brand-new leg, how could she fail?

Two tankards clinked together, some froth was slopped and two voices giggled, cackled and guffawed in that order.

Doctor Residue was talking proudly and loudly to his friend 'Admiral' Colin Blotch, a small man in a small uniform with a small brain. The so-called Admiral had been hit on the head by a cannonball years before. Now he

could not even tie his shoelaces
without a chart. He stared at the
tankard and tried to remember what
to do with it.

Doctor Residue swallowed a
hearty mouthful and Colin copied.

'See, that leg has a history. That
leg was not always a leg. That leg
was made from a truncheon, once
owned by Captain Gruff McHanley,
the famous press-ganger. For years
he stalked the streets of Portsmouth,
finding innocent young men and
forcing them into a lifetime at sea!

184

You've heard of him?' asked the doctor.

Colin thought long and hard about the question and said, 'No.'

Mr Blackbarrel was fighting a losing battle with his piano as the doctor embarked on the final leg of his tale.

'It is said the ghost of old McHanley still haunts the truncheon – the same truncheon I made into a leg and sold to Dame Peggie Slops.'

He giggled. Colin giggled too.

'It is also said that whenever McHanley heard a certain sound he went into a mad frenzy of head-hitting, attacking people from here to the Thames.'

Colin slurped a final gob of froth from his tankard and said, 'What sort of sound?'

Suddenly, Mr Blackbarrel had his groaning piano under control and launched into a merry dance tune loved by the folk of the Cluttered Plughole. A huge cheer went up, drowning out Doctor Residue's final words.

'*Music! Dance music!*'

That night the Cluttered Plughole was more cluttered than ever before. Word had spread, sentences had seeped and whole paragraphs had leaked: this was the night of the Pirate Ball.

The walls were festooned with bunting and the flags of all nations. A fine feast lay across the longest table in the tavern — pilchard

187

trifle, prawn
ice cream,
whale-tail
on toast

and octopus dippers for the kids.

Mr Blackbarrel had dusted off his silver bow tie for the evening and was tinkling away in the corner on his newly tuned piano. If the music sounded awful only his fingers could now be blamed.

The party was in full swing and the roar of the crowd was deafening; everyone was having the jolliest of jolly times. (Everyone except one small woman by the name of Mary Celeste, who was banging her empty tankard on the bar, trying – and failing – to attract the barman's attention. She was getting very annoyed.)

Already folks had entered the dancing contest. Claude and Maude D'Courcy had wowed the audience with their triple fandango and Betty Ricketts had performed a sizzling break-dance in which she'd broken a lot of things – a

189

fingernail, a jug of lemonade and the record for oddest dance of the competition.

Each contestant was judged by a po-faced pirate, Mrs J. T. Butterbox. She had a chalkboard on which she scribbled marks out of ten. So far, she looked as bored as a plank.

'Ladles and diddle-men,' Mr Blackbarrel announced eventually, 'my have I you untension? Is there any more dancering people wishing to sally forth on the dance flow and do us a diddling dance?'

Faces looked at faces that looked at faces that looked at faces. Everyone who wished to dance had, it seemed, danced.

'Very welly then! I shall ask the budgie to—'

'Wait!'

A hooded figure which had silently appeared in the corner whisked off its hood and revealed itself to be –

'Dame Peggie Slops!' croaked the barman. 'She always knows how to make an entrance!'

The light tinkled off her tiara. Her newly polished teeth gleamed in her mouth. Her dress trickled with jewellery. She struck a pose in the centre of the room and waited.

Mr Blackbarrel coughed. He leaned forward, shielding his eyes from the glittering costume, and said, 'I doughnut have any music!'

The beer tap dripped in expectation. Everyone waited. Dame Peggie was frozen in the glare of every eye in the room.

The silence was broken by a

small woman banging her tankard on the bar. It was Mary Celeste again.

'Beer!' she shrieked.

Ambrose Click, the oldest barman this side of the Nile, ambled over and held his hand to his ear.

'Eh?'

'I want a can of beer to take away!'

'Eh?' he said again.

She suddenly breathed deeply and bellowed loudly, 'Can! Can!'

'Oh, a cancan!' said Mr

193

Blackbarrel, leaping back on his stool and grabbing the piano like it was about to escape. He began belting out the tune to the best of his abilities.

Dame Peggie Slops stood as still as a clipper without a whiff of wind. This was not the music she had rehearsed to. What was she to do? She looked at the expectant faces and decided to give it a go.

Dame Peggie spun and span and twirled and turned. She dipped and doffed, tangoed, foxtrotted and cha-

194

cha-chaed. All to the sound of the cancan! The amazed eyes of the Cluttered Plugholers widened with each dazzling step.

Mrs J. T. Butterbox began muttering to herself and even smiled.

Then things started to go wrong.

'Ooooooooooooooooooooooooooo ooooooooooooooooooooooo!!!!'

It was a moaning groan! No one seemed to know where it was coming from, but everyone could hear it. Then Dame Peggie

195

gasped as she felt her wooden leg twitching under her dress. Suddenly, without warning, it performed a dance move she had not rehearsed. Except it wasn't a dance move. The wooden leg was actually dragging Dame Peggie towards Mrs Butterbox.

Step by step she moved closer, step by step she tried to resist. The spectators all held their breath as Dame Peggie was dragged closer and closer to the judge. No one realized that the music was causing

the chaos and Mr Blackbarrel,
thinking he could quell the madness,
played even louder.

The hopping Dame Peggie was
led along until the leg was within
clouting distance of the judge. It
appeared from under Dame Peggie's
beautiful white dress like a cannon
raising up and spotting its target.
And its target was Mrs Butterbox.

With one swift swat the leg
swiped – and missed! Mrs Butterbox
whooped and whimpered and ran
for the door.

The leg scanned the room and poor Dame Peggie pivoted on the spot. It was looking for another victim and soon located Mr Blackbarrel. Once again, poor Dame Peggie was dragged along, this time towards the gulping musician. By now she had come to her senses and shouted, 'Pull it off! Pull it off!' But the audience hadn't come to its senses and didn't know what to pull off.

The leg clunked towards the stage.

199

Mr Blackbarrel could do nothing except play louder and louder.

The leg got closer and closer.

It dragged Dame Peggie up the steps, on to the stage and across to Mr Blackbarrel. Inches away from the musician's sweating head, it hovered in front of his crossed eyes.

Suddenly Mr Blackbarrel grabbed the wooden leg, placed it under his arm and swirled Dame Peggie Slops across the dance floor. They stood silently, the appendage finally stilled by the lack of music. But the contest had to continue, and so the barman whipped from beneath the bar a small, portable gramophone player. A huge brass horn protruded from the top, and a handle dangled from the side. He slid it across the damp bar to Mary Celeste (who was still waiting for her beer). She stared at it in bewilderment and said, 'Is this a wind-up?'

'Yes!' hissed the barman. 'Turn the handle!'

And she did. And from the brass horn pumped a joyful dance tune

201

that nobody's feet could resist.
Dame Peggie and her partner
started tapping theirs, then slapped
their hands and finally launched
into a full-flung dance routine.

They ducked and dived and spun
and span. Dame Peggie performed
the steps she had rehearsed and Mr
Blackbarrel kept her haunted leg
under control.

'Ooooooooooooooooooooh!' said
the leg, starting to sound a little
confused.

As the dance finished, the crowd

roared its approval and Dame Peggie finally removed her leg. All three took a bow.

'Oooooooooooooooooooooh!' As the leg started to twitch and tremble once more, Mr Blackbarrel snatched it from Dame Peggie and hurled it through the tavern window. All fell silent in the room until the distant splash of the plopping leg was heard – at which point a huge cheer went up!

The barman climbed up on to his bar and declared to the merry

203

masses, 'Dame Peggie Slops, ladies and gentlemen. I think you will agree with me when I say that was the finest performance of the cancan ever seen on these shores!' He started to clap and one by one all the Plugholers joined in and the clapping became cheering and the cheering became stomping. And in the midst of the clapping, cheering and stomping the barman strolled over to the judge's empty chair and picked up the first prize: a bright, shiny golden cup on which was printed:

204

For the
FINEST SEA LEGS
on
DRY LAND

He presented the cup to Dame
Peggie Slops, who was breathless,
gobsmacked and a little confused.
But she gracefully received the
award and agreed to pose for an
oil painting for the local gallery.
She even slipped
her arm around Mr
Blackbarrel.

The rest of the
evening was spent in

a rollicking, jollisome swirl of fun and frolics. Each and every pirate there would one day tell the tale of the time they witnessed the dance of Dame Peggie Slops and her Haunted Wooden Leg.

The Ghost Ship

Roger Stevens

'Where are you going, Jake?'

My sister Sally has a way of popping up when you don't want her to.

'Shhh,' I say, 'I don't want Mum to hear.'

207

'But it's getting dark. And it's nearly supper-time.'

'I know. If Mum asks where I am, tell her I've gone to the shop for some . . . um . . . football cards. I won't be long.'

I go out the back door and creep round the house to the alley. Then I'm running; past the new houses, down to the coast road. As I reach the beach the breeze from the sea wants to knock me down and the air's wet with the salty spray. It's high tide and the sound of the surf crashing into the shingle is deafening. I turn left and follow the promenade towards the cliffs.

When I reach the cliff path Dan, my best mate, is waiting for me.

'You took your time,' he says.

'Mum kept asking about school,' I say. 'I had to wait for her to go upstairs.'

We climb the cliff path. It's dark now, but you can just make out the line of the chalky path, snaking between the brambles and thistles and exposed flints. Above us looms the black shape of the huge bonfire. We've been building it for over a week now, and loads of people have helped. It's the biggest bonfire you've ever seen. Everyone thinks we built it for November the Fifth.

We put it about two-thirds of the way up the hill, in a slight dip in the cliff, but where it will be seen clearly from the town below –

and from the sea. We couldn't build it on the cliff-top because the winds would blow it down again.

Dan and I stand at the base of the huge pile of branches, old boxes, broken furniture, pallets and all sorts of other junk and I think about all our friends and their parents who helped us build it and all the hard work that everyone put into it and I really hope we're doing the right thing.

We take the old newspapers from Dan's bag and scrunch and screw

211

up the pages and go round the fire, poking them between the sticks and branches.

I look at my watch. It's twenty-six minutes past four.

'OK, let's do it,' I say.

I'm feeling nervous. What if it doesn't light? And what will everyone say when they see it burning – four days too early? Dan and I will be in serious trouble if anyone finds out it was us.

Now Dan is going round the base of the huge wooden pile with his matches, lighting the paper. The fire takes hold really quickly and the crackling flames, fanned by the wind, are soon racing skywards.

I walk to the cliff edge and stare out to sea, scanning the horizon. And I'm thinking back to another night like this: the night of the great storm.

It was one year ago. I missed the bus after school and decided to walk home. If I miss the bus I'm supposed to call Mum to fetch me in the car.

But I was angry. I'd been told off by Mad Frank the PE teacher for leaving school by the 'IN' door, and I needed to cool off.

As I reached the top of the cliff path a jagged streak of lightning fizzed across the sky. It was already dark at half past four, and only the beginning of November. The lightning was followed by an almighty clap of thunder that shook the ground.

I stood at that highest point on the cliffs and stared out to sea.

There was a gale blowing up and I felt as if I was going to topple over. The sea was rough, with high foam-flecked waves. Below me I could see the town of Seamouth and the little rows of street lanterns that lit my road. Any minute now the rain would come and I knew I'd better hurry before I got drenched – or worse, hit by lightning.

I was about to run home when I saw something out at sea. I peered into the gloom. It was a ship, sailing dangerously close to the

215

submerged rocks around the coast.
It was heading straight towards the
peninsula, where the cliffs and rocks
stretch out into the sea like jagged
white teeth.

There was another flash of
lightning. I gasped. In the bright
white light I could see that this
was no ordinary ship. It was a
sailing ship – one of those big, old-
fashioned ones with high white sails.
I watched with growing horror
as the ship rose and fell, heading
slowly for the rocks.

Then, it climbed to the top of a
particularly high wave and seemed
to freeze in mid-air. And the wind
was suddenly quiet, as though it
was holding its breath. There was
another flash of lightning and I saw
the strangest thing of all – the skull-

and-crossbones flag. This was a pirate ship!

The ship fell. And, despite the noise of the sea crashing against the cliffs and the roar of the wind, I could hear the shivering crunch of the ship as it broke in two. I watched in horror. Then there was another clap of thunder and the rain started.

'Hey! Boy!'

A voice behind me made me jump. There stood a tall figure silhouetted against the flashes of lightning that arced across the sky. He was dressed in ragged clothes with a red scarf wound round his head. His face was ghostly white. There was a gold earring in his ear and fire in his eyes. In his hand was a cutlass – and it was pointing at me.

I turned and sprinted down the path, slipping and sliding in the mud. I heard his voice chasing me on the wind:

'Wait! Boy! Stop!'

★

There was a knock at the door. It was the coastguard — a large man wearing a heavy raincoat and carrying a big yellow umbrella. He propped the dripping brolly next to the fridge and hung his coat on the back door while Mum poured him a cup of tea.

We all sat round the kitchen table.

'Well, well, well,' said the coastguard. 'So you're the lad who saw the ship go down?'

'I thought we should call you,' Mum said. 'When Jake got home he

220

was in a terrible state. Was it bad?
We've had the news on but there's
been nothing yet.'

'Well, we did check out your
boy's story,' the man said slowly.
'And you know what? There was
no sign of a wreck — we searched
all along the shore. There were no
boats in that area.'

'You're wrong!' I cried. 'I saw it.'

'No sign of a wreck,' the
coastguard said again. 'Maybe with
all that rain and sea spray you were
mistaken.'

'No!' I shouted, 'I really did see it!'

At that moment the phone in the hall rang. Mum excused herself and went to answer it, leaving me and the coastguard alone at the table.

'Don't worry,' the man said, getting up, 'I won't report you for wasting everybody's time.'

'But I *saw* it,' I said. 'It was terrible. It kind of hung there on the crest of a wave and the . . . and the . . .' I felt close to tears.

'Was it an old-fashioned pirate ship by any chance?'

'Yes, it was!' I cried. 'But . . . how did you know?'

'A ship *did* go down off the coast there — but it was hundreds of years ago. It was called the *Black Doubloon*.'

'You what?'

The coastguard drained his cup of tea and started putting on his raincoat. 'Well, you're not the first to have seen it.'

'Are you telling me I saw a ghost ship?'

He opened the back door and a gust of cold, wet wind blew in, sending a shiver down my spine.

He winked at me. 'Don't be ridiculous. Oh, and thank your mum for the tea.'

At school the next day I told Dan all about it. During IT we looked up the *Black Doubloon* on the Internet and, sure enough, it had existed. It was indeed a pirate ship and hundreds of years ago, on November the First, it had hit the rocks off the peninsula and sunk. Apparently some of the remains — an old cannon and some cannonballs — were on display in the town museum.

After school we decided to walk home along the cliff path. There was a stiff breeze, although nothing like the wind on the night before.

'It was out there,' I told Dan, pointing.

'Well, there's no sign of a wreck,' he said. 'How weird. Maybe it's because—'

'Wait. What's that?' I interrupted. It sounded like someone crying out for help.

We both listened. But the sound had gone.

'Perhaps it was another ghost,' Dan said hopefully.

'Maybe,' I said. 'But it was probably just a seagull.'

'Maybe it was the ghost of a seagull!'

'Dan,' I said, 'now you're being silly.'

★

That night I woke up from a nightmare in which I had been fighting pirates, duelling on the rigging with my sword. But then they captured me and forced me to walk the plank. I was just about to fall into the sea when I woke up.

I lay there in the dark, thinking about the dream and about the shipwreck. As I listened to the wind outside, I could almost feel the room swaying.

But wait. The room *was* swaying. It was moving – up and up, pausing and then swooping back down. I could feel the motion in my stomach. And I could hear weird creaking noises coming from the walls and ceiling of my room.

I could also hear voices – but not the voices of my parents or my sister. It sounded like two men talking. One said something about bad visibility, and then I heard the other say, quite clearly, 'What was that? There's someone there.'

I heard footsteps and in the doorway stood the pirate with the red scarf — the one I'd seen on the cliff. He came towards me, grinning, as I scrambled under the duvet to hide . . .

'Jake, Jake, wake up.'

I opened my eyes. It was Dad.

'Did you have a bad dream? You were shouting.' He tucked me in, gave me a kiss and said goodnight. Afterwards I lay awake for a while, listening to the wind.

At school I told Dan all about the dream.

'I wish I had dreams like that,' he said, 'I'd love to see a ghost.'

'No you wouldn't,' I said. 'It was horrid. It was like the pirate was really in my room.'

'I saw a programme about ghosts once,' Dan said. 'And the thing is – ghosts are troubled souls who get trapped between this world and the next one. They have to keep doing the same things over and over again. It's like being in a prison. And they need a way to break out so that their souls can be laid to rest.'

I thought about what Dan had said all morning and then, at lunchtime, when Mad Frank was telling someone off for coming in through the 'OUT' door, I had my brilliant idea. And I hatched my plan.

So Dan and I are on the cliffs and the bonfire has really taken hold. It's a fantastic fire, and flames and sparks are leaping up to the clouds. Over the roar and crackle of it all I can hear someone yelling, and I can see torch-beams coming up the cliff path. The fire's been seen from the town. We're going to be in big, big trouble.

We stand as close as we dare to the edge of the cliff, and stare out to sea. I check my watch. Four thirty exactly. I'm sure that was the time I saw the ship last year. But what if I'm wrong?

I can hear people running up the path now and shouting. *What's going on? Who lit the fire?* Then, just

232

beyond the line of jagged rocks that disappear into the ocean, I spot it.

'There it is! Can you see?'

'Yes,' says Dan. 'I can. I *can* see it. It's the ghost ship. Wow!'

More people arrive. No one can believe that the fire has already been lit. But Dan and I are just staring out to sea, watching the ghostly white sails of the *Black Doubloon* billow in the wind. And as we watch, the ship slowly changes course and turns away from the

233

rocks. It doesn't crash into them this time. It sails safely past and finally the ghostly galleon disappears from sight. I know we won't be seeing it again.

Dan grins at me and I grin back and we turn to the fire. The heat is tremendous.

'Look,' whispers Dan.

There, just beyond the orange glow of the fire, stands a pirate. He has a red scarf wound round his head and a gold earring. He raises his cutlass in salute, winks at us

both, and then, like smoke from the
fire, he's gone.

Handy Guide to Pirate-speak

(Because you never know when you might need it . . .)

Pirate word/phrase:	What it means:
ahoy there	hey
avast ye	stop and pay attention
aye	yes
be	am or are, as in 'I be', 'you be', 'they be' . . .
bilge rat	pirate insult (the 'bilge' is the darkest part of the ship, just below the floorboards of the bottom level)
black spot	if you are 'marked with the black spot' you are under a death threat

booty	treasure
buccaneer	pirate who preyed on Spanish shipping in the West Indies in the seventeenth century

cat-o'-nine-tails	whip used for punishment
corsair	pirate who roamed the Mediterranean Sea
dance the hempen jig	to hang
Davy Jones's locker	pirates believed that Davy Jones was an evil spirit who lurked in a realm at the bottom of the sea – his 'locker': where their souls would end up when they died

doubloon	Spanish gold coin
gentlemen o' fortune	polite name for pirates
grog	rum-based pirate drink
here be dragons	section of a map showing uncharted territory
Jolly Roger	the skull-and-crossbones pirate flag
landlubber	literally 'land lover' – someone not very good on board a ship

lily-livered	cowardly

Handy Guide to Pirate-speak

matey	shipmate
me hearty	my friend
nay	no
ne'er	never
piece of eight	Spanish silver coin
privateer	captain of an armed vessel

scurvy	disease caused by not having enough vitamin C in your diet – pirates were at risk because they didn't usually have fruit and vegetables on board ship
scurvy dog	another pirate insult
ship's biscuit (or 'hard tack')	dry type of bread designed for long-term storage
shiver my timbers	pirate exclamation of surprise
swashbuckling	fighting with swords
weevil	type of beetle which often attacks grain stores

Six Famous Pirates

Ann Bonnie

Ann Bonnie was an Irish woman who lived in the eighteenth century – a time when superstition stated that having women on board ship brought bad luck. Despite this, Ann ran away to the Caribbean with pirate Calico Jack Rackham, captain of the *Revenge*. Another woman, Mary Read, became a pirate in their crew. (Stories say she disguised herself as a man to do it.)

Blackbeard

Blackbeard was the nickname of Edward Teach – an English pirate who terrorized the Caribbean in about 1717. Legend says that when he attacked ships he tied slow-

burning fuses into his long black beard and set them alight. Many merchants were so petrified by the smoking flames around Blackbeard's face, together with his blood-thirsty reputation, that they surrendered immediately.

Captain Hook

The villain in J. M. Barrie's story *Peter Pan*, he wears an iron hook instead of his right hand, which was cut off by Peter Pan and fed to a crocodile. The crocodile liked the taste so much that it follows him around, hoping for more. Captain Hook's ship is the *Jolly Roger* and his blundering first mate is Smee.

Captain Jack Sparrow

In the *Pirates of the Caribbean* films, Captain Jack Sparrow was captain of the *Black Pearl* – until Hector Barbossa led a mutiny and took the ship from him. Captain Barbossa took the crew of the *Black Pearl* to find the legendary treasure of Cortez – which

cursed them all never to die. Jack Sparrow finally defeated Barbossa and reclaimed his ship, before going on to have many other adventures . . .

Long John Silver

A fearsome pirate in the story *Treasure Island* by Robert Louis Stevenson. He has a peg leg and a parrot called Captain Flint, who perches on his shoulder.

Sir Francis Drake

Francis Drake was an Englishman born in 1540. On his galleon, the *Golden Hind,* he raided Spanish ships in the Caribbean seas and acquired enormous wealth. On just one attack he amassed eighty pounds of gold, twenty tons of silver, thirteen cases of silver coins and cases full of pearls and precious stones. He brought his plunder back to Queen Elizabeth I and she rewarded him by making him a knight!

Acknowledgements

The compiler and publisher wish to thank the following for permission to use copyright material:

Philip Ardagh for 'Spilt Milk' by permission of the author; **Ian Billings** for 'Dame Peggie Slops and her Haunted Wooden Leg' by permission of the author; **Fiona Dunbar** for 'Beaky McCreaky, Parrot of the High Seas' by permission of The Agency (Ltd) London on behalf of the author; **Cornelia Funke** for 'Pirate Girl', first published in the UK by Chicken House in 2005, by permission of the author; **John Grant** for 'Uncle Jolly Roger' by permission of the Elizabeth Roy Literary Agency on behalf of the author; **David Harmer** for 'The Treasure of Shark's Tooth Island' by permission of the author; **Colin McNaughton** for 'The Pirats' by permission of the author; **Vic Parker** for 'Pirates Win Prizes' by permission of the author; **Roger Stevens** for 'The Ghost Ship' by permission of the author; **Anna Wilson** for 'Captain Whiskers and the Fishy Tail' by permission of The Agency (Ltd) London on behalf of the author.

Pirate

Poems

by David Harmer

A splendid volume of swashbuckling verse

The One They Feared the Most

Morgan made them walk the plank
Ann Bonnie danced on dead men's bones
Bonnet flew the Jolly Roger
Rackham sailed with Davy Jones.

William Fly hanged them high
Crazy Mary sank them fast
Edmund Low stole their gold
Thomas Tew smashed their mast.

Moody blew their boats to bits
Rackham set their sails on fire
Kennedy cut off their ears
Cutlass Liz was vile and dire.

But the one they feared the most
Was Old Blackbeard, Edward Teach
He taught them all the dance of death
On their final, rocky beach.

THE RAT WITH THE HUMAN FACE

THE QWIKPICK PAPERS

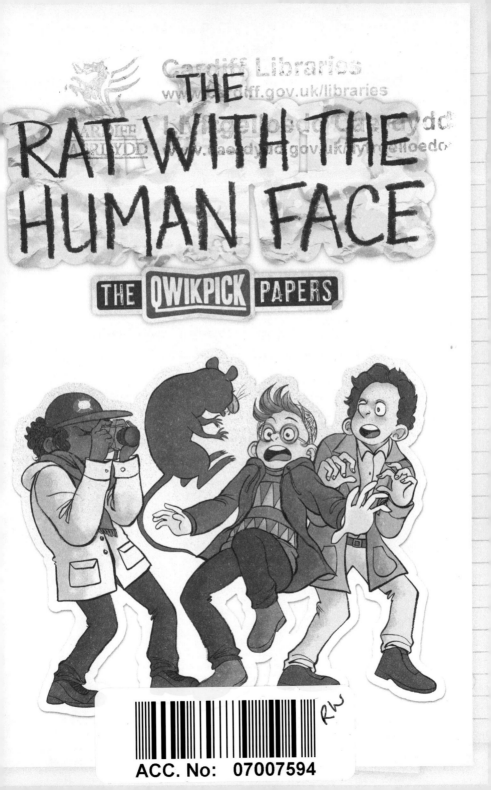

Books by Tom Angleberger

In the Qwikpick Papers series
Poop Fountain!
The Rat with the Human Face
To Kick a Corpse

In the Origami Yoda series
The Strange Case of Origami Yoda
Darth Paper Strikes Back
The Secret of the Fortune Wookiee
Art2-D2's Guide to Folding and Doodling
The Surprise Attack of Jabba the Puppett
Princess Labelmaker to the Rescue!
Emperor Pickletine Rides the Bus

In the Inspector Flytrap Series
Inspector Flytrap
Inspector Flytrap in The President's Mane Is Missing

Fake Mustache
Horton Halfpott

For younger readers
McToad Mows Tiny Island

Amulet Books
New York